For Julia

John Gruen

Flowers & Fables

paintings by

Rafal Olbinski

design by

Rita Marshall

For Cathy and James —
you are lovely
dreamers....

Love
John Gruen

Creative Editions

mankato

Harcourt Brace & Company

san diego   new york   london

Mimosa

AN old, old woman sat in a white and gold room sur-

rounded by her four daughters. She looked at them one

by one. The eldest daughter, she noted, rested her hands

atop her head as if weary of them. The next-to-eldest

daughter stood facing an oval mirror, a deep and secret

smile forming on her lips. The third daughter moved her

head slowly to-and-fro as if she could not grasp some-

thing. The fourth daughter – the youngest and fairest of

them – twined mimosa in her hair. The old mother rose,

walked toward her youngest child, untwined the fronds of

mimosa that trembled in her hair, and whispered, "Now the

mimosa shall weep her golden tears in an old woman's hands."

A violent wind lifted a silver mirror toward the cloud-filled sky. Moving upward, the mirror resembled a gleaming white bird lancing the fierce wind. Soon it grew dark and a sound like bells brushing against glass could be

V i o l e t

heard in the distance. This sound was the shattering of the silver mirror. And where the glittering rain of the mirrored pieces fell, an infinity of violets transformed the landscape into a soundless perfumed sea.

IN a very still orchard where sunlight and shadow formed

intricate patterns, a small child sat playing. His game was

changing butterflies into sweet peas, and sweet peas into

butterflies. Soon the child tired of the game. As he turned

S w e e t P e a

to leave the orchard an odd sensation came over him. He

felt his arms turning into soft pale wings and his body into

a tender yet firm green stem. He cried out, but no one heard

him. As night began to fall, a garland of mauve butterflies

fluttered about the curiously changed child, and suddenly

he took wing and flew sadly and quietly toward the moon.

IT was snowing heavily. The child walked slowly through

the white silence of the snowfall. An old man stopped the

child. "Do you know why it snows?" he asked. "No,"

answered the child. The old man looked deeply into the

Star of

Bethlehem

child's eyes and said, "It is because each driving snowflake

is very angry. You see, it realizes that as it is falling, it can nev-

er be the tiny flower it actually believes itself to be – the Star

of Bethlehem. All it ever manages to shape is a very white,

very soft memory of what that snowy flower looks like."

AT dusk, when nightingales begin their song, a special

color falls upon all flowers. This color has no name, but

those who have seen it say that it brightens each flower it

touches—that it makes each lily whiter, each rose deeper.

M a r s h
M a l l o w

It does this for every flower except one. When this magic

color falls on the marsh mallow, its fragile petals tremble

and mysteriously vanish. Only at dawn do stem, leaf,

and petal reappear, casting a dim blue shadow on the

moist and dewy ground.

ON an unknown and oddly shaped island, two creatures

with long flowing hair sat amidst thousands of carnations.

They neither talked nor sang nor slept nor ate. The only

thing they ever did was stare and stare at each other. One

Carnation

day a storm came up, and the two strange creatures were

swept out to sea. Moving swiftly along the waves, they

appeared as two statues. Their long golden hair formed a sail

on the horizon. The wind carried them into endless nights

and days, and it was the remembered scent of carnations

that continued to keep their gaze fixed upon each other.

NO one would say it. No one would admit that the

grass had turned gray or that the cedars had fallen or that

the poplars had slowly and majestically risen to the sky.

Everyone continued to stare at the stark, silent sea laven-

Sea Lavender

der. They did not know that to stare so long at so sweet

and awkward a bloom meant the rearrangement of things

in nature. Everyone stayed transfixed as the sea lavender

slowly and imperceptibly wove itself about the heads of

those who questioned its powers.

P o p p y

A young princess lay dreaming on a soft mound of poppy blossoms. Silently, a long silken bird came upon the sleeping princess. His small, brilliant eyes blinked twice, and twice again. Then, spreading his pearly wings, he hopped onto the lovely dreamer, covering her pale face with the soft down of his outspread wings. The princess stirred and smiled softly. Now, all around them, the poppy blossoms swayed very gently, making a sound like distant harps. But a great and fierce wind rose, causing a rain of poppy petals to fall and cover both bird and princess. And as the wind subsided, the air grew moist and a pale mist began to form, hiding princess, bird, and blossoms – leaving only a memory of their shape and fragrance.

IN a distant land, some travelers stopped near a brook.

Its waters were cool and of many colors. One of the travelers, a boy with large gray eyes, threw some rocks into the brook. While the rocks slowly sank into the water,

A n e m o n e

the skies darkened, and a pale rain began to fall. Suddenly, the travelers were turned into cypress trees – all, that is, except the young boy, who moved slowly into the quiet waters of the brook. Floating all around him were strange and beautiful flowers. These were called anemones.

The boy sank slowly, dreaming their colors.

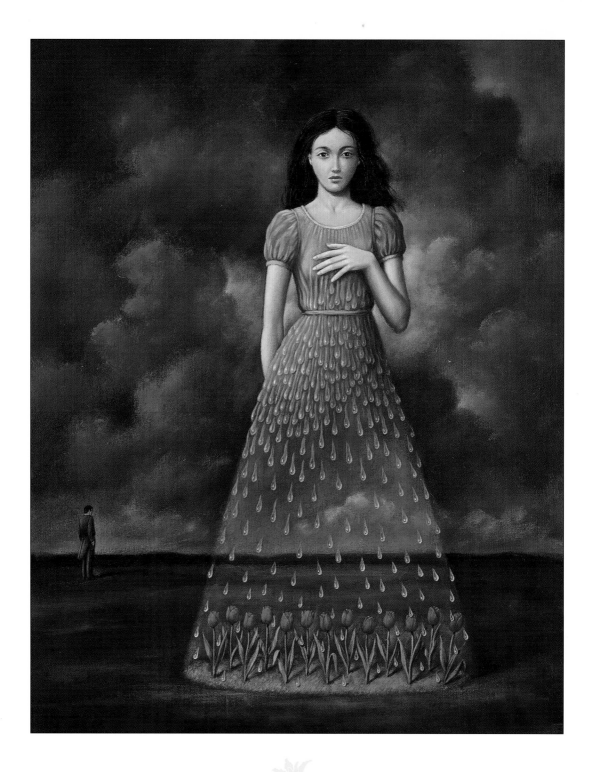

T u l i p

IN Persia, there lived Tulipa. She sprang from the tears

of her young lover, Ferhad, a Persian youth of great wealth

and beauty. Legend has it that Ferhad once dreamed of a

maiden so perfect, so loving and gracefully formed, that he

set out on a voyage to find her. After many years of wan-

dering, he came upon a quiet field. The wind made no

sound. The sky was still. The grasses and wildflowers did

not stir. Ferhad's heart began to break. He remembered his

love so clearly, but could not find her. And so he wept for

his love. Where his tears fell there sprang a lovely blossom,

and out of the blossom sprang Tulipa. But Ferhad never

saw his perfect love. He had already died of sadness.

THE queen placed the crown upon her head. The prin-

cess held a yellow fan to her lips. The young prince lifted

his chalice high. The king rose to his feet. The merchants

brought their silks. The jewelers, their pearls. The luta-

Lilac

nists plucked their strings. The dancers curved their

arms. The servants bowed their heads. When the Moor

struck his tiny cymbals, everyone froze in place. It was

at this moment that the lilac in the royal gardens burst

into bloom, and everyone in the palace whispered the

word: *Listen!*

BEHIND a closed door could be heard the sound of many children laughing. There was such glee and such joy behind that closed door that no one ever dared open it for fear that all that happiness might vanish. One day,

Bachelor Button

someone knocked on the door. At first the laughter continued as before. But as the knocking grew more urgent, the laughter subsided and soon stopped altogether. The silence behind the door became as dense and as blue as a bachelor button, while the knocking, which did not cease, had the cruel, insistent sound of that miraculous flower.

THE emperor of a long and ancient dynasty summoned

his only daughter to his music chamber. There, amidst gold

and ivory instruments, he bade her sing a sweet, sad melody—

one he had, as a youth, often sung himself. As the young

I r i s

princess began the song, the old emperor's eye caught the

reflection of an iris trembling softly against the shiny sur-

face of a golden bowl. As his eyes fixed upon the image of

the flower, he realized that his lovely daughter had long

since died, and that the melody he was hearing came from

deep within him, like the distant music heard in dreams.

W i s t e r i a

A moss-green tower stood near a dense, shadowy wood.

One night, a child on horseback, having lost his way, came

to the entrance of the tower. Dismounting, the child walked

up to the immense door and rapped on it with all his might.

After a long while, the door slowly and creakily opened.

Before him stood a tall creature shrouded in wisteria.

Swiftly and decisively, the child tore at the wisteria, pulling

its sinewy green ropes and leaves with all the strength he

could summon. But the more he tore and pulled, the more

entangled he himself became in the pungent blooms. Soon,

the pulling child and the tall, silent creature merged into one,

while nearby the waiting horse sank to the ground with a

great and mournful shudder.

Requests for permission to make copies of any part of the work
should be mailed to: Permissions Department,
Harcourt Brace & Company, 6277 Sea Harbor Drive,
Orlando, Florida 32887-6777.

Creative Editions is an imprint of The Creative Company,
123 South Broad Street, Mankato, Minnesota 56001.

Library of Congress Cataloging-in-Publication Data
Gruen, John.
Flowers & fables/John Gruen: illustrated by Rafal Olbinski.
Summary: A collection of fourteen short fables
each of which describes a different flower.
ISBN 0-15-201311-3
1. Fables. [1. Fables. 2. Flowers--fiction.]
I. Olbinski, Rafal, ill. II. Title.
PZ8.2.G69F1 1996 [Fic]-dc20 95-45738

First edition A B C D E

Color Separations by Photolitho AG, Gossau
Printed in Italy by Grafiche AZ, Verona